Y0-BTW-090

EPISODE I

ADVENTURES

GAME BOOK

The Ghostling Children

Dave Wolverton

LUCAS BOOKS

SCHOLASTIC INC.

New York Toronto London Auckland Sydney
Mexico City New Delhi Hong Kong

ISBN 0-439-12988-5

12 11 10 9 8 7 6 5 4 3 2 1   0 1 2 3 4 5 6/0

Printed in the U.S.A.
First Scholastic printing, January 2000

For the full story behind your adventure, read up to page 61 in your Star Wars Adventures novel, *The Ghostling Children*. Or begin here.

You are Anakin, Kitster, Dorn, or Pala. The *Adventure Guide* contains the rules of Star Wars Adventures. You must follow these rules at all times.

Sebulba's henchmen have kidnapped some Ghostling children. These children are being held in the fortress of Gardulla the Hutt, an evil slave trader. At dawn, doctors will place exploding transmitters inside the children, making them slaves forever.

You and your friends are disguised as Jawas. You cannot let yourselves be seen or caught. You must break into Gardulla's fortress and sneak down into the slave pens beneath. Once there, you must deactivate the alarms in the main security room so that you can free the Ghostling children. Then you must get them to safety.

Choose your character. Every character has unique talents that are listed on each character card. You can use Power three times on this adventure.

You start this adventure with your Adventure Point (AP) total from your previous adventure, or 1000 AP if this is your first adventure.

May the Force be with you.

YOUR ADVENTURE: RESCUE THE GHOSTLING CHILDREN

You and your friends silently streak over the hardpan on your sand skimmers toward Gardulla's fortress, hugging the shadows beside a pile of rocks. Red lights on the fortress dome make you think of bloodshot eyes — searching, searching.

It reminds you of the fact that there are guard droids on the wall whose only purpose is to emit a shrill whistle if anything odd approaches.

Ahead, a narrow chasm splits the rocks, where desert winds have eroded a passage. An adult on a speeder couldn't make it through, but it is just the right amount of space for a kid on a sand skimmer.

"Keep your heads down," you whisper to your friends. "There's razor moss growing on the rocks."

You glide through the narrows of the chasm. Long white funnel flowers protrude from crevices above, making soft breathing noises as they inhale the night air, trying to get moisture.

You kick the ground and build up speed. Rock walls to either side seem to fly past. Here and there, hubba gourds grow on the ground. Their faceted husks reflect the starlight.

You round a turn. Something big and dark huddles on the trail. At first you think a boulder has fallen, but the thing lifts an ugly head. It emits a fierce growl.

"Cliffborer worm!" you shout to the others.

Cliffborer worms come out on Tatooine at night. They feed on razor moss and suck water from hubba gourds. With one good bite, a cliffborer worm could suck you dry. After that, you'd just be food for the gravel maggots.

You can choose to evade the cliffborer worm without Power, evade it with Power, fight it with a sleep-dart, or fight without a sleep-dart.

To evade the cliffborer worm (without Power): Roll the 20-dice to veer from the path of the monster. The number you roll is your roll#. If navigation is one of your talents, your roll# + your navigation# + your vehicle's stealth# + 1 is your adventure#. If navigation is not one of your talents, your roll# + your navigation# + your vehicle's stealth# is your adventure#.

If your adventure# is equal to or more than 13, add the difference + 7 to your AP total. You slip past the cliffborer worm as easily as snot slips from a Hutt's nose. You may proceed.

If your adventure# is less than 13, subtract the difference from your AP total. The cliffborer worm lunges and knocks you from your sand skimmer. Your sleep-darts fall out of your hand. You must get them back. Roll the 10-dice. Your new roll# + your stealth# is your new adventure#.

> *If your new adventure# is equal to or more than 6,* add 1 AP to your AP total. You reach your sand-skimmer and your sleep-darts. Before the cliffborer worm can make another attack, you jump on the sand skimmer and take off.

> *If your new adventure# is less than 6,* subtract the difference from your AP total. You manage to get to your sand skimmer and your sleep-darts — but the cliffborer worm is on top of you before you can escape. You must fight it, either with or without the sleep-darts (page 9).

To evade the cliffborer worm [with Power]: Choose your Reflex Power. Roll the

20-dice to veer from the path of the monster. The number you roll is your roll#. Your roll# + your vehicle's stealth# + your Power# + your Power's low-resist# is your adventure#.

If your adventure# is equal to or more than 13, add the difference + 7 to your AP total. You slide past the cliffborer worm so fast that it nearly ties itself in a knot trying to get a look at you. You may proceed.

If your adventure# is less than 13, subtract the difference from your AP total. The cliffborer worm lunges and knocks you from your sand skimmer. You must either run from the worm (below), fight it with your sleep-darts (next page), or fight it without sleep-darts.

*NOTE: This counts as one of three Power uses you are allowed on this adventure.

To run from the worm: Roll a 10-dice to evade on foot. Your roll# + your strength# is your adventure#.

If your adventure# is equal to or more than 6, add the difference to your AP total. You scream and jump around, somehow managing to slip past the worm and regain your sand skimmer. You may proceed.

If your adventure# is less than 6, subtract the difference from your AP total. The cliffborer worm takes a nasty bite out of you. You will need medical attention when you get into the fortress. Until then, subtract 1 from your strength#. The cliffborer worm is now through with you, so you may proceed.

To fight the cliffborer worm (without sleep-darts): Roll the 20-dice to pick up a rock and hurl it at the worm. The number you roll is your roll#. Your roll# + your strength# + your skill# is your adventure#.

If your adventure# is equal to or more than 13, add the difference + 7 to your AP total. The rock slams into the worm's head and knocks it silly. You may proceed.

If your adventure# is less than 13, subtract the difference from your AP total. The rock misses its target. Go back to "Roll the 20-dice to pick up a rock" and repeat until you have defeated the worm.

To use a sleep-dart: Roll the 20-dice. The number you roll is your roll#. Your roll# + your weaponry# + your weapon's mid-range# is your adventure#.

If your adventure# is equal to or more than 14, add the difference + 7 to your AP total. The worm takes a sleep-dart right in the eye and falls to the ground as if it had miraculously turned into rubber. You may proceed.

If your adventure# is less than 14, subtract the difference from your AP total. Your shot misses wildly. You'll have to try again. Go back to "Roll the 20-dice" and repeat until the worm is defeated.

You make it past the cliffborer worm and hurtle through the narrows until at last the canyon opens into a small valley.

"Keep to your left," you call to the others. "Stay in the shadows. We're right under the fortress walls."

You hardly need to tell them. Above you the fortress looms, a black monolith in the night. Red lights from windows high overhead gleam evilly. You can hear faraway music, Kloo horns that wail like human screams, drifting from a darkened room.

Now you slow your sand skimmer, creeping, until the cliff meets the wall of Gardulla's fortress.

You dismount directly below a round hole

twenty meters up. It's a vent that lets hot air escape the castle. There are iron bars on the vent, meant to keep everyone out. One of the bars has been sawed through, making a hole big enough for a child to climb through. As part of your plan, a grappling hook is wedged between two iron bars.

You reach out and feel along the wall.

To find the grappling hook's fibercord: Roll the 10-dice. If tracking is one of your talents, your roll# + your skill# + 2 is your adventure#. If tracking is not one of your talents, your roll# + your skill# is your adventure#.

If your adventure# is equal to or more than 6, add the difference + 5 to your AP total. You find the fibercord, and may proceed.

If your adventure# is less than 6, subtract the difference from your AP total. All you can feel is wall. Then a tiny spydr jumps onto your hand. Shake it off before it bites! Roll the 10-dice. Your new roll# + your stealth# is your new adventure#.

If your new adventure# is equal to or more than 5, add the difference to your AP total.

11

You flick the spydr off. One of your friends points out the fibercord, and you may proceed.

If your new adventure# is less than 5, subtract the difference from your AP total. OUCH! The spydr bites you, then scurries back onto the wall, chittering happily. One of your friends points out the fibercord, and you may proceed.

"Here," you whisper. You find the reel on the ground and hook it to your belt.

You hear an electronic whir up above, atop the wall. You all flatten against the wall just as a guard droid wheels to a stop. You hear its hydraulics as it turns its mechanical head, peering over the ledge.

You hold your breath, terrified that the droid will see one of you. You must avoid detection, with or without Power.

To avoid detection (without Power): Roll the 10-dice to hide in the shadows. Your roll# + your stealth# is your adventure#.

If your adventure# is equal to or more than 7, add the difference + 6 to your AP total. You're as hard to spot as a grain of sand in a Tatooine desert. You may proceed.

If your adventure# is less than 7, subtract 5 AP from your AP total. The droid makes a grinding noise in surprise. You will have to blast the droid with the ion blaster to keep it quiet (next page).

To avoid detection (with Power)*: Choose your Infiltration Power. Roll the 20-dice to hide in the shadows. Your roll# + your Power# + your Power's mid-resist# + your stealth# is your adventure#.

If your adventure# is equal to or more than 13, add the difference + 6 to your AP total. You're as hard to spot as a grain of sand in a Tatooine desert. You may proceed.

If your adventure# is less than 13, subtract the difference from your AP total. The droid makes a grinding noise in surprise. You will have to blast the droid with the ion blaster to keep it quiet (next page).

*NOTE: This counts as one of three Power uses you are allowed on this adventure.

To blast the guard droid: Roll the 10-dice. Your roll# + your weaponry# + your ion blaster's mid-range# is your adventure#.

> *If your adventure# is equal to or more than 7,* add the difference to your AP total. The droid gives a small electronic screech before it shuts down. You may proceed.

> *If your adventure# is less than 7,* subtract the difference from your AP total. The droid lets out a high-pitched wail of alarm. You must silence it. Roll the 10-dice again. Your new roll# + your weaponry# + your ion blaster's mid-range# +1 is your new adventure#.

>> *If your new adventure# is equal to or more than 7,* add 2 AP to your AP total. The droid gives a small electronic screech before it shuts down. You may proceed.

>> *If your new adventure# is less than 7,* subtract the difference from your AP total. The droid is on to you. Go back to "Roll the 10-dice again" and repeat until you have silenced the droid.

You have gotten past the guard droid. But you must be careful — there could be others around. You must quickly and quietly scale the wall, using the grappling hook.

To scale the wall: Roll the 10-dice. Your roll# + your stealth# + your strength# + is your adventure#. (If you were injured by the cliffborer worm, remember to subtract 1 from your strength#.)

If your adventure# is equal to or more than 8, add the difference + 6 to your AP total. You hook the electric reel to your belt and silently glide up the wall.

If your adventure# is less than 8, subtract 5 from your AP total. You hook the electric reel to your belt and go clattering up the wall so loudly that you sound like a rusty droid. Proceed with caution — the guard droids may have heard you.

You reach the shaft for the vent. You and your friends wiggle between the iron bars and climb inside.

For making it into the fortress, reward yourself with 60 APs.

You have to crawl for a long way, past the kitchens and the laundry rooms, past the sleeping quarters for Gardulla's henchmen. You slide down a side chute to the pool room.

Here, Gardulla keeps several large swimming pools, some with waterfalls and fountains. She often swims in one of the pools when Tatooine's dry air gets to her. Other times she likes to stock a pool with carnivorous fish and have her guards toss in anyone who has displeased her.

You sit quietly for a moment to listen before you enter the room. You doubt that anyone would be here at this time of night, but you can't take a chance. A grate fits over the vent, and you can't see past it. Glowrods near the ceiling give off only faint light.

Every sound echoes through the room. Waterfalls tumble softly. Your hear the skittering feet of a big insect.

You figure that if the shy bug is foraging for dinner, the room has to be empty.

The air smells heavily of water. You wait for the others to reach you. You whisper, "If we get split up, let's meet back here."

You hope that you'll all be able to find

your way back if you get split up. The corridors down here in level six are a maze. When the hill was mined, the miners struck off in any direction they wanted. There are side tunnels that lead nowhere, empty rooms, switchbacks, and dead ends.

Gardulla keeps the new slaves penned down here partly because it is such a maze. It's hard to escape.

You open the grate quietly and drop to the ground. You step away to make room for the next person, then crouch. The others leap down behind you.

Overhead, glowrods near the high ceiling look like slivers of stars. Potted plants beside the pools form a screen between you and the water. In some places, huge boulders have been placed for decoration.

You slink beside a pool, quietly making for the main door. Behind you, someone's shoes squeak.

"Hmmmm?" a deep voice bellows from the water nearby. Something huge stirs in the pool, making a splash.

There, floating on her back, is Gardulla the Hutt!

"Who's there?" she demands in Huttese.

The Hutt is wallowing in the shallows like a small whale. Her enormous head is propped up on a rock, her eyes closed to slits. She's half asleep.

Behind you, the others come to a halt. Someone's feet slap loudly on the pavement.

You can't hide, since Gardulla knows that you are in the bushes. But you can't just run for it either, since she would call her numerous guards.

You must keep Gardulla quiet. You can try to talk your way past her, with or without Power. Or you can try to put her to sleep with a sleep-dart.

To talk your way past Gardulla the Hutt (without Power): Roll the 20-dice to convince her that you are a servant passing through. To do this, you must talk nicely and not let her see beneath your hood. If charm is one of your talents, your roll# + your charm# + 3 is your adventure#. If charm is not one of your talents, your roll# + your charm# + your stealth# is your adventure#.

If your adventure# is equal to or more than 15, add the difference + 15 to your AP total. Gardulla believes that you are a servant and asks you to scrub her back. Proceed to scrub Gardulla's back (next page).

If your adventure# is less than 15, subtract the difference from your AP total. Gardulla recognizes that you are a fake. Proceed to the section that begins with "Gardulla shouts in alarm" on page 23.

To talk your way past Gardulla the Hutt (with Power)*: Choose your Persuasion Power. Roll the 20-dice to convince her that you are a servant passing through. To do this, you must talk nicely and not let her see beneath your hood. Your roll# + your charm# + your Power# + your Power's high-resist# is your adventure#.

If your adventure# is equal to or more than 13, add the difference + 15 to your AP total. Gardulla believes that you are a servant and asks you to scrub her back. Proceed to scrub Gardulla's back (next page).

If your adventure# is less than 13, subtract the difference from your AP total. Gardulla recognizes that you are a fake. Proceed to the section that begins with "Gardulla shouts in alarm" on page 23.

*NOTE: This counts as one of three Power uses you are allowed on this adventure.

To hit Gardulla with a sleep-dart: Roll the 10-dice. Your roll# + your weapon's mid-range# + your weaponry# is your adventure#.

If your adventure# is equal to or more than 8, add the difference + 12 to your AP total. You're lucky to have such a big target. Unfortunately, even though you hit her, the sleep-dart doesn't do much to quiet something as enormous as Gardulla. Proceed to the section that begins with "Gardulla shouts in alarm" (page 23).

If your adventure# is less than 8, subtract the difference from your AP total. You miss Gardulla. The dart lands right next to her. She notices, and yells to her guards. Proceed to the section that begins with "Gardulla shouts in alarm" (page 23).

To scrub Gardulla's back: Roll the 20-dice to lift the enormous brush. It's as long as a Wookiee and feels like it weighs almost as much as you do. Your roll# + your skill# + your strength# is your adventure#. (Note: if you got bitten by the cliffborer worm, remember to subtract 1 from your strength#.)

If your adventure# is equal to or more than 15, add the difference + 10 to your AP total. You do a good job scrubbing Gardulla's back.

20

Flakes of her skin, along with various bugs and parasites, fall into the water. As you scrub, your friends all sneak out the door of the pool room. However, all of this work makes Gardulla hungry. "Hmmm, that felt good," Gardulla booms in Huttese. "But now I want a little something to eat. How about you?" Proceed to the section that begins, "Gardulla decides to eat you" (below).

If your adventure# is less than 15, subtract the difference from your AP total. As you scrub Gardulla's back, your hood falls off your head. Gardulla yells to her guards. Proceed to the section that begins with "Gardulla shouts in alarm" (page 23).

Gardulla decides to eat you. She reaches up to grab your ankle.

You must evade Gardulla, with or without Power.

To evade Gardulla (without Power): Roll the 10-dice to leap from her grasp. Your roll# + your strength# + 1 is your adventure#. (If you were injured by the cliffborer worm, remember to subtract 1 from your strength#.)

If your adventure# is equal to or more than 7, add the difference + 5 to your AP total. You leap like a lizard from Gardulla's slimy grasp. Proceed to the section that begins, "Gardulla shouts in alarm" (next page).

If your adventure# is less than 7, subtract the difference from your AP total. Gardulla's strong hands have you firmly by the ankle. She drags you toward her mouth. You must fight (next page).

To evade Gardulla (using Power)*: Choose your Jump Power or your Reflex Power. Roll the 10-dice to leap from Gardulla's grasp. Your roll# + your strength# + your Power# + your Power's mid-resist# is your adventure#. (If you were injured by the cliffborer worm, remember to subtract 1 from your strength#.)

If your adventure# is equal to or more than 8, add the difference + 5 to your AP total. You bound from Gardulla's grimy grasp. Proceed to the section that begins, "Gardulla shouts in alarm" (next page).

If your adventure# is less than 8, subtract the difference from your AP total. Gardulla's vise-like hands have you firmly by the ankle. She drags you toward her mouth. You must fight (next page).

*NOTE: This counts as one of three Power uses you are allowed on this adventure.

To fight Gardulla the Hutt: Roll the 20-dice to squirt cleanser down Gardulla's smelly throat. Your roll# + your strength# + your stealth# is your adventure#.

> *If your adventure# is equal to or more than 14,* add the difference + 3 to your AP total. You squirt the cleanser into the monster's gullet. Gardulla begins to choke. Her enormous tongue comically lolls from her mouth. She shouts, "Poison! Ah, it's poisoned me! Guards!" Proceed to the section that starts, "Gardulla shouts in alarm" (below).

> *If your adventure# is less than 14,* subtract the difference from your AP total. Gardulla continues to drag you — kicking and screaming — toward her mouth. Go back to "Roll the 20-dice to squirt cleanser down Gardulla's smelly throat" and repeat until you get some soap down her throat.

Gardulla shouts in alarm. Your heart is pounding as you race from the pool room into the main access tunnel. Your friends are already there.

The main corridor is simply a rough rock wall, painted white. It winds through the hill like a serpent. There are side passages everywhere, many with big security doors bolted crudely over the openings.

You quickly search for your exit.

A door flings open on your right. A Gamorrean guard thuds into the hall, stun baton drawn.

Your friends all scream, then run from the guard.

You follow them. The guard is right behind you. His armor jangles. He sounds like a tank driving down the hall. You know you'll never get away fast enough. You run around a corner and hide. You must either try to trip the guard or fight him with your sleep-darts.

To trip the Gamorrean guard: Roll the 20-dice. Your roll# + your strength# + your stealth# is your adventure#.

If your adventure# is equal to or more than 14, add the difference + 9 to your AP total. Your foot expertly connects with the guard's armored ankle. It feels as if your own leg will rip off, but the guard falls with a sound like a load of garbage spilling from a lifter. You may proceed.

If your adventure# is less than 14, subtract the difference from your AP total. The guard hits your leg — but doesn't fall. Instead, he turns to you, ready to attack. Fight him with your sleep-darts (below).

To throw a sleep-dart: Roll the 10-dice. Your roll# + your weapon's short-range# + your weaponry# is your adventure#.

If your adventure# is equal to or more than 8, add the difference + 7 to your AP total. The dart sinks deep into the guard's flesh, and he's off to dreamland! You may proceed.

If your adventure# is less than 8, subtract the difference from your AP total. The guard sees the dart and cringes in fear. Roll the 10-dice again. Your new roll# + your weapon's short-range# + your weaponry# + 1 is your new adventure#.

If your new adventure# is equal to or more than 8, add the difference + 7 to your AP total. The dart sinks deep into the guard's flesh, and he's off to dreamland! You may proceed.

If your new adventure# is less than 8, subtract the difference from your AP total. The guard sees the dart and cringes in fear. Go back to "Roll the 10-dice again" and repeat until the guard goes nighty-night.

You run until you reach a T in the hallway. You turn to see several droids marching toward you, fresh from an oil bath.

"Ah!" a golden protocol droid cries on seeing your group. "Jawas! And they have an ion blaster." The droid raises its hands over its head and begins hopping around in terror.

"Please, don't shut me down," the protocol droid begs. "My gyro balance circuitry will be thrown off for days! Here, have my locomotor — I'll give you anything you want."

The droid begins to open its forward access panel.

You may ignore the droid, or you may use your ion blaster to shut all the droids down.

To ignore the droids and walk past: Roll the 10-dice to walk past without causing a disturbance. Your roll# + your stealth# is your adventure#.

If your adventure# is equal to or more than 7, add the difference + 12 to your AP total. You pass the droids without difficulty, and may proceed.

If your adventure# is less than 7, subtract the difference from your AP total. As you pass, you hear one of the droids say, "Call security at once!" You must shut the droids down (below).

To shut down the olly droids: Roll the 20-dice to fire the ion blaster. Your roll# + your weapon's short-range# + your weaponry# is your adventure#.

If your adventure# is equal to or more than 14, add the difference + 8 to your AP total. The protocol droids stop in their tracks. You may proceed.

If your adventure# is less than 14, subtract the difference from your AP total. You've shut down a couple of the droids, but a few more remain. Go back to "Roll the 20-dice to fire the ion blaster" and repeat until all of the droids have stopped working.

Distantly, you hear the voice of Gardulla the Hutt, booming through the hallways. "Guards! Get them!"

This isn't going the way you thought it would.

Gardulla is after you. Distantly, echoing

down the hall, you hear the boots of pursuing guards, and the clang of armor.

As you rush along, you spot a door marked BUG RANCH.

You open the door. Inside you see row after row of cages. They are filled with enormous bugs. Lots of them. There are poisonous ghost spydrs from Kubindi, bigger than some houses you've seen. There are giant two-headed effrikim worms — a Hutt's favorite snack — three meters long. There are mora beetles with giant horns on their noses, pounding their cages.

Obviously, these aren't normal bugs. You remember hearing that Gardulla has a gourmet chef from Kubindi, one who specializes in cooking insects. But of course such a chef wouldn't use just any insects. These have been bred for size and tastiness, and probably have been fed chemicals and growth serums to make them mutate into gigantic form.

The stink of alien bugs makes your nose itch. The insects began to hiss and chitter. The beetles blow a noise from their horns that sounds like, "Flee. Flee."

You suddenly realize that these bugs could make a great diversion.

You run to the control panel for the cages.

To open the bug cages: Roll the 20-dice. If lock bypass is one of your talents, then your roll# + your skill# + 4 is your adventure#. If lock bypass is not one of your talents, your roll# + your skill# + 1 is your adventure#.

If your adventure# is equal to or more than 12, add the difference + 5 to your AP total. The cages glide open. Ghost spydrs, mora beetles, and horrible two-headed worms all leap out, looking for the nearest victim. You may proceed to run away as fast as you can.

If your adventure# is less than 12, subtract the difference from your AP total. You haven't been able to open the cage. Taking a deep breath, you try again. Roll the 20-dice a second time. If lock bypass is one of your talents, then your new roll# + your skill# + 4 is your new adventure#. If lock bypass is not one of your talents, your new roll# + your skill# + 2 is your new adventure#.

If your new adventure# is equal to or more than 12, add the difference to your AP total. The cages glide open. Ghost spydrs, mora beetles, and horrible two-headed worms all leap out, looking for the nearest victim. You may proceed to run away as fast as you can.

If your new adventure# is less than 12, subtract the difference from your AP total. Still no luck. Go back to "Roll the 20-dice again" and repeat until you've opened the cage.

As you run from the bug ranch, you spot a Gamorrean guard down the hall. At that moment, a huge mora beetle crashes into the main corridor, its nose horn blaring, "Flee! Flee!"

It slams against the wall of the corridor, and looks as if it might just sit and batter itself for awhile. Then it catches sight of the Gamorrean.

The beetle wheels, lowers its nose horn, and charges the guard.

The Gamorrean screams. He turns and runs, grunting with every stride.

You watch the giant beetle ram the guard from behind. The Gamorrean slides on his belly and hits the wall headfirst, driving his iron helmet over his eyes. The giant beetle charges around a corner, looking for its next victim.

You whisper under your breath, "And I thought *my* house had bug problems!"

The Gamorrean guard crawls to his knees, and tries to pry the cap off his head.

You turn and flee.

You race through the maze of tunnels until you near the slave quarters. There, you reach the security booth where all of the alarms and monitors for the slave pens are controlled.

You know that you can't break into the slave's infirmary without taking control of the booth.

You punch a button to open the security booth. The door slides up. A horribly scarred man in a dark gray uniform is sitting at a desk. Above him is a bank of monitors that show images of some of the main corridors and rooms in the fortress. On one of the monitors, you see the giant bugs escaping from their pens.

"Oh, no!" the guard is muttering. "The bugs are out!" He's reaching for a red button marked ALARM.

You must stop the guard from pushing the alarm. You try to persuade him to stop (with or without Power), attack him without a weapon, attack him with the sleep-darts, or blast the control panel with the Jawa ion blaster.

To persuade the guard to not sound the alarm (without Power): You tell the guard that if he sounds the loud alarm it will only make the bugs act crazier. You tell him you are from the local Jawa bug capture unit, and that things will soon be under control. Roll the 20-dice. If either communication or charm is one of your talents, your roll# + your charm# + 2 is your adventure#. If neither communication nor charm is not one of your talents, your roll# + your charm# is your adventure#.

If your adventure# is equal to or more than 12, add the difference + 4 to your AP total. The guard nods and takes his hand away from the alarm. You may proceed. Go to "You run to the slave infirmary" on page 39.

If your adventure# is less than 12, subtract the difference from your AP total. The guard doesn't buy your story. Proceed to use your sleep-darts to put him to sleep, or your ion blaster to disable his console (page 35).

To persuade the guard not to sound the alarm (using Power)*: Choose your Persuasion Power. You tell the guard that if he sounds the loud alarm it will only make the bugs act crazier. You tell him you are from the local Jawa bug capture unit, and that things will soon be under control. Roll the 20-dice. Your roll# + your charm# + your Power# + your Power's mid-resist# is your adventure#.

If your adventure# is equal to or more than 13, add the difference + 4 to your AP total. The guard nods and takes his hand away from the alarm. You may proceed. Go to "You run to the slave infirmary" on page 39.

If your adventure# is less than 13, subtract the difference from your AP total. The guard doesn't buy your story. Proceed to use your sleep-darts to put him to sleep, or your ion blaster to disable his console (page 35).

*NOTE: This counts as one of three Power uses you are allowed on this adventure.

To attack without a weapon: Roll the 20-dice to launch yourself at the guard in a flying tackle. Your roll# + your strength# + your stealth# is your adventure#.

If your adventure# is equal to or more than 15, add the difference + 5 to your AP total. You slam into the guard like a freight train, and the poor fellow bangs his head against his computer console. You may proceed. Go to "You run to the slave infirmary" on page 39.

If your adventure# is less than 15, subtract the difference from your AP total. The guard leaps aside and draws his weapon. Proceed to the section that begins with "The guard fixes you with his beady eyes" (next page).

To attack with the sleep-darts: Roll the 20-dice to aim and throw. Your roll# + your weaponry# + your weapon's close-range# is your adventure#.

If your adventure# is equal to or more than 14, add the difference + 4 to your AP total. The dart lodges in the guard's button-pushing finger. You can bet he'll be dreaming of revenge for the rest of the night. You may proceed. Go to "You run to the slave infirmary" on page 39.

If your adventure# is less than 14, subtract the difference from your AP total. The guard snarls like a womp rat. Proceed to the section that begins with "The guard fixes you with his beady eyes" (below).

To disable the control panel with the Jawa ion blaster: Roll the 10-dice to hit the button to shut everything down. Your roll# + your weapon's short-range# + your weaponry# is your adventure#.

If your adventure# is equal to or more than 9, add the difference + 6 to your AP total. Blue rings of ionized energy bathe the room. Electricity flashes over the console. The monitors above the guard's head explode in a flash of colors. Proceed to the section that begins with "The guard fixes you with his beady eyes" (below).

If your adventure# is less than 9, subtract the difference from your AP total. You need more practice. The blue ionized rings strike the security guard. He goes cross-eyed for half a second. "What the . . . ?" he wonders aloud. Proceed to the section that begins with "The guard fixes you with his beady eyes" (below).

The guard fixes you with his beady eyes. "You dirty little Jawas!" he shouts. "What are you doing here?"

The guard reaches for his blaster and pulls it from his holster. You stare down the barrel, and for one instant, an instant that stretches into endless torment, a torment that yawns wider than Dune Sea, you realize that your life is about to end.

Images flash from your short life as a slave on Tatooine. They aren't all bad. You recall walking with your friends along a canyon, picking up small polished agates called "Bantha tears."

You remember the most beautiful sunrise on a day when the sands held a shimmer that had been kissed by starlight. Twin suns the color of a rose soared over the far hills and painted Tatooine's jagged canyons in shades of pink so exquisite you felt as if the color had somehow pierced you, as if it had been stained behind your eyes.

You recall a day so hot that Jira, the kindly old juice vendor, took pity on you and gave you a dimma freeze for free. It was the most satisfying drink you ever had.

In that moment, as the guard draws his blaster on you, your short life seems sweet and miraculous. There is so much left to experience, so much to be savored.

Wait a minute! you tell yourself. *What am I doing just standing here?*

It's true that time slows when you're facing death. But you suddenly recognize that it doesn't freeze forever. If you don't do something quick, the guard will blow your brains out!

So you do the only thing you can think to do: you reach for the CLOSE button on the door. You may close the door with or without Power.

To close the door (without Power): Roll the 10-dice to punch the CLOSE button. Your roll# + your skill# + 2 is your adventure#.

If your adventure# is equal to or more than 7, add the difference + 25 to your AP total. The door whisks closed.

If your adventure# is less than 7, subtract 15 AP from your AP total. You stand like a womp rat in the headlights of a speeder as your death approaches. Luckily, you have some friends who think faster than you. One of them shoves you aside and closes the door.

To close the door (using Power)*: Choose your Alteration Power or your Reflex Power. Roll the 10-dice to activate the CLOSE button. Your roll# + your skill# + your Power# + your Power's mid-resist# is your adventure#.

If your adventure# is equal to or more than 8, add the difference + 25 to your AP total. The door whisks closed.

If your adventure# is less than 8, subtract 20 AP from your AP total. You stare open-mouthed as your death approaches. Luckily, you have some friends who think faster than you. One of them shoves you aside and closes the door.

*NOTE: This counts as one of three Power uses you are allowed on this adventure.

The door slams down just as the guard pulls his trigger.

You hear the pinging sound of the blaster bolt ricocheting through the room. Then there is groan, followed by a dull thud as the security guard plops to the floor.

"Oh no," you breathe in terror. "I hope he's not dead!"

If you get caught now, you're in terrible trouble.

You run to the slave infirmary.

Farther back in the fortress, you can hear Gamorreans yelling and blasters firing. Someone has discovered the giant bugs. That will keep Gardulla's guards busy!

You must get the infirmary door open. It has an electronic lock that can only be opened if you punch in the proper combination. The door is so thick that you can't knock it down. You must bypass the lock.

To bypass the lock: Roll the 20-dice. If either repair or lock bypass is one of your talents, your roll# + your skill# + 2 is your adventure#. If neither repair nor lock bypass is one of your talents, your roll# + your skill# is your adventure#.

If your adventure# is equal to or more than 12, add the difference + 10 to your AP total. The door to the infirmary opens. You may proceed.

If your adventure# is less than 12, subtract the difference from your AP total. Go back to "Roll the 20-dice" and repeat until you get the door open.

It is dark inside the infirmary. Tanks, lighted from beneath and filled with bacta, bubble in one corner. Beds fill the middle of the room.

In another corner is the energy cage, with the Ghostling children inside. The cage looks like a simple black platform, but a shimmering blue haze surrounds it. The Ghostling children are all lying on the platform, sound asleep.

For finding the Ghostling children, add 80 AP to your AP total.

In front of the cage stands a guard — a great big giant cyclops from the planet Byss.

The giant scrutinizes you with its huge eye, and growls in its best approximation of Huttese, "Hey, what are you Jawas doing here?"

Your heart freezes. You don't know much about giants from Byss, but you have heard a few things. They are practically impossible to kill, and they are as dumb as rocks.

You may try to bluff your way past the

guard, or you may attack the guard with your sleep-darts.

To bluff your way past the guard: You stride to the front of the door, trying to look confident. In a high voice, as if you are a Jawa who has somehow mastered Huttese, you answer, "You go. We guard prisoners now." Roll the 10-dice. If communication is one of your talents, your roll# + your charm# + 4 is your adventure#. If communication is not one of your talents, your roll# + your charm# + 2 is your adventure#.

If your adventure# is equal to or more than 8, add the difference + 10 to your AP total. The cyclops opens its eye wide in delight. "Really? You'll let me go early?" He lumbers out the door, much to your relief.

If your adventure# is less than 8, subtract the difference from your AP total. This cyclops is smarter than he looks. It's time to use your sleep-darts (below).

To use your sleep-darts: Roll the 20-dice. Your roll# + your weapon's mid-range# + your weaponry# is your adventure#.

If your adventure# is equal to or more than 13, add the difference + 8 to your AP total. The cyclops gets hit in the chest. It laughs at you, and says, "It takes more than a little bitty dart like this to hurt me!" He strides toward you, and then says, "Good night, Mommy." He does a nosedive to the floor. You may proceed.

If your adventure# is less than 13, subtract the difference from your AP total. The cyclops watches the dart whiz past, and says in a booming laugh, "Oh, I'm really scared." He steps toward you. Roll the 20-dice again. Your new roll# + your weapon's mid-range# + your weaponry# + 2 is your new adventure#.

If your new adventure# is equal to or more than 13, add the difference to your AP total. The cyclops gets hit in the chest. It laughs at you, and says, "It takes more than a little bitty dart like this to hurt me!" He strides toward you, and then says, "Good night, Mommy." He does a nosedive to the floor. You may proceed.

If your new adventure# is less than 13, subtract the difference from your AP total. You must try again. Go back to "Roll the 20-dice again" and repeat until the giant has fallen.

You rush over to the cage. Its lock looks very sophisticated. As you kneel to study it, one of the Ghostling children stirs in her sleep — the girl Arawynne.

She glances up at you and instantly comes awake. She carefully disentangles herself from the children she has been holding. She tries to get up, but she is badly bruised. She gasps in pain. As she climbs to her feet, the children begin to stir. "Wake up," she tells them. "We're getting out of here!"

You watch the children in rising concern. The Ghostlings are frail. They've had a rough trip here, and all of them are badly bruised and injured. You had imagined that they would all run off with you, but Arawynne can hardly move.

You hear the sound of booted feet out in the hallway. Some Niktos are shouting in their crude language, listening to a communicator.

One of your friends closes the door. You all kneel quietly as the Nikto guards approach.

You can hear part of the Niktos' conversation over the communicator as they sprint past. "There's a mora beetle chasing Mistress Gardulla around in the pool," someone warns the guards. "And watch the south corridor. Ghost spydrs are stringing webs everywhere!"

You are trembling. You had hoped to sneak into the compound quietly and save the Ghostling children without anyone knowing. Now the whole fortress is as busy as a Ferrelian anthive.

"Oh no," one of your friends says as he kneels by the door. "We just locked ourselves in."

"Here, get me out of this cage," Arawynne grumbles. "I know how to get us out of this room!" In spite of her injuries, Arawynne shows a lot of spunk.

You must open the energy cage. You can open the cage with or without Power.

To open the cage (using Power)*: Choose your Alteration Power. Roll the 20-dice. Your roll# + your skill# + your Power# + your Power's mid-resist# is your adventure#.

If your adventure# is equal to or more than 15, add the difference + 10 to your AP total. The shimmering field around the energy cage disappears. You may proceed.

If your adventure# is less than 15, subtract the difference from your AP total. Power isn't working here. Try to open the cage without Power (below).

*NOTE: This counts as one of three Power uses you are allowed on this adventure.

To open the cage (without Power): Roll the 20-dice. If either repair or lock bypass is one of your talents, your roll# + your skill# + 3 is your adventure#. If neither repair nor lock bypass is one of your talents, your roll# + your skill# + 1 is your adventure#.

If your adventure# is equal to or more than 14, add the difference + 10 to your AP total. The blue energy field disappears. You may proceed.

If your adventure# is less than 14, subtract the difference from your AP total. Go back to "Roll the 20-dice" and keep trying until you get the cage open.

Arawynne and the Ghostling children are free!

Award yourself 50 AP points.

If the cliffborer worm injured you, you can now heal yourself using the emergency medical supplies here in the infirmary.

To heal yourself: Roll the 10-dice. (NOTE: You only need to do this if you were injured by the cliffborer worm earlier.)

If you roll 1, 2, 3, or 4: Subtract 10 AP from your AP total. You are healed, and your strength# returns to normal.

If you roll 5 or 6: The infirmary doesn't have the medicine you need. You must continue to subtract 1 from your strength# for the rest of this adventure.

If you roll 7, 8, 9, or 10: You are healed, and your strength# returns to normal.

Now you have to get the Ghostlings to safety.

"How can we get out of here?" you ask Arawynne.

"Blow the door open!" Arawynne answers.

Blowing the door open sounds dangerous. Someone might get hurt. Besides, it is sure to attract unwanted attention. So far,

Gardulla doesn't know why Jawas would be in her fortress, causing trouble. But once this door blows, she'll be after you.

"Blow it open with what?" you ask.

"Look over on the counter. There's a box of transmitters," Arawynne says. She points to a small box on the counter. They are the transmitters that Gardulla's doctor planned to put in Arawynne and the others. "We can use them to blow up the door."

You run to the box. The transmitters are small wafers about the size of your thumbnail. The black exterior is made of axidite, and a set of numbers is painted on it.

A white component to the transmitter houses some circuitry. This piece has a small receiver in it. That way, when Gardulla sends a signal to the transmitter telling it to blow up, it will blow up.

There are dozens of transmitters in the box. With them is a transmitter that carries the numeric codes.

Boy, you think, *I sure wish I could put one of these transmitters in Gardulla. If I did, she'd treat everyone better from now on!*

You pick up a transmitter, memorize the number, and carry it to the door. You wedge the wafer between the door and wall, up by the electronic lock.

"Everybody watch out!" you tell the others. You get the little transmitter and push in the code numbers. You hide behind an operating table and make sure that everyone else is also well-hidden. You push the SEND button.

The transmitter roars. Flame fills the passageway, and the door evaporates into dust. Smoke fills the room.

A smoke alarm begins blaring. "Breeep. Breeep. Breeep."

You raise your head above the operating table, and stare wide-eyed at the gaping hole. Now you know what you would look like if the transmitter that your master has planted in your own body ever exploded.

"Hurry!" Arawynne shouts. "We have to get away from here before the guards come." She begins herding the Ghostling children from the room as fast as she can.

You grab the box of transmitters, shoving them into your pocket. They might come in handy later.

You quickly lead the children to a nearby elevator. As the door closes, you hear the sound of boots rushing down the hall toward the infirmary.

With the guards coming down to level six, the best thing to do is to take the elevator up, away from the danger. But that would just leave you all stranded higher up on the mountain.

Even a short run has left the Ghostlings out of breath. They are from a world where gravity is far lighter than it is on Tatooine. They'll never be able to run all the way to the exit. They'd never be able to make the trip to town.

And you doubt that you can carry them. It's too dangerous. Even touching one of the Ghostlings leaves them bruised.

You look up and catch Arawynne's attention. "Where to?" she asks.

"Maybe we can fly out of here," you say. You press the elevator button and take it up six floors.

"You're crazy," one of your friends objects. "We can't fly!"

"We've got to find some way to get the Ghostlings to safety," another one says.

The elevator stops, and the door opens into the hangar for the spaceships. You are under the huge dome of the fortress. There are dozens of ships here: Corellian freighters, light cruisers, even a couple of Z-95 headhunters. Maintenance droids are working singlemindedly to fuel and clean the ships.

The domed roof, which can open to let ships in and out, is closed for the night.

You study at the dome, the ships sitting quietly. "It won't work," you tell them. "We'd have to get the dome open in order to fly out. And as soon as we tried, Gardulla's gunners on the towers would shoot us down. We'll have to find another way."

You look back at Arawynne. One of the Ghostlings, a small boy, is sobbing. You've come so far to help them, but you can't see an easy way out.

"How far do you think you can run?" you ask. It is a long way from here to the vent, where you hope to escape.

"We can't go much farther," Arawynne answers.

One of your friends suggest, "We'll have to hide them for now, come back later. Where can we hide them?"

You think quickly. There are dozens of places — one of the spaceships nearby, or one of the storage rooms. But those areas would be searched first, and most thoroughly. Besides, there is no telling how soon you can come back to get them.

One of your friends says, "I've got an idea. Come with me!"

He leads the group across the flight deck, and through a hallway beyond. "I figure that with bugs downstairs — and Jawas, and explosions — everyone in the fortress will be looking for us down there. But there is one place that they won't suspect!"

All you need to do is find the right door.

To find the right door: Roll the 20-dice. If tracking is one of your talents, your roll# + your skill# + your stealth# + 2 is your adventure#. If tracking is not one of your talents, your roll# + your skill# + your stealth# is your adventure#.

If your adventure# is equal to or more than 15, add the difference + 5 to your AP total. You find the right door, and may proceed.

If your adventure# is less than 15, subtract the difference from your AP total. You open a door — but it's the wrong door! You are now facing the Gamorreans' sleeping quarters. The room is filled by the sound of gruntlike snoring. You must quietly close the door before they notice you are there. Roll the 10-dice. Your new roll# + your stealth# is your new adventure#.

If your new adventure# is equal to or more than 6, add the difference to your AP total. You close the door gently. Now go back to "Roll the 20-dice" and repeat until you've found the right door.

If your new adventure# is less than 6, subtract the difference from your AP total. One of the Gamorreans stirs. You pause before you can close the door. When the Gamorrean has safely started to snore again, you must try once more to close the door. Go back to "Roll the 10-dice" and repeat.

You reach a huge iron door and press a button.

The door whisks open, and with it comes the smell of fresh air and trees, water, moss, and rocks. The dome above is covered in transparisteel that lets in the starlight. In that light, you can see the twisting trunks of trees. Huge luminous moths dance in the air above some flowering vines. Fans stir the air, and in the distance you hear running water.

"This is Gardulla's pleasure garden," you say.

"But," one of your friends objects, "aren't there animals in here that eat people?"

"Not yet," another friend says. "Not for months. Gardulla's foresters aren't done. They've been working all season, planting trees and flowers, and now they're almost done. They're Ho'Din."

The Ho'Din are a peaceful people from the planet Moltok. Their very name, Ho'Din, means, "Walking flowers." They are tall and lean, with gorgeous red and violet scales that hang from their heads like hair. They love nature.

You would be willing to bet your own life that the Ho'Din would help hide the Ghostlings. Indeed, you *are* betting the lives of the Ghostling children.

Something pale, like an ugly spydr, crawls toward your group through the door.

"No animals?" one of your friends says. "I wouldn't go in there with that."

"That's not an animal," Arawynne corrects. The Ghostling Princess kneels to examine the thing. "It's more like a seed, sort of — a seed that walks. It pulls itself off of a gnarltree. Then it goes looking for a place to plant itself."

"We can't have the children stay here," one of your friends says. "It's spooky."

"If there are trees," Arawynne replies, "then it will feel like home. There will be good places to hide, down among the roots. I can't think of a place I'd rather be."

"We'll come back for you," you promise Arawynne and the children. "We'll bring you food. And when all the excitement dies down, we'll figure out how to get you home."

Arawynne stares at you and your friends — her rescuers — for a long moment, and chokes back a sob. "Thank you," she says in a husky voice. "Thank you." She gathers the children and leads them into Gardulla's pleasure garden.

Now, you must escape the fortress.

You take winding tunnels through long-forgotten mining shafts and grimy air vents.

It seems that everyone in Gardulla's fortress is awake and searching for you. You're constantly running, hiding from the sounds of approaching guards.

You're afraid that someone will come up behind you, so every once in awhile, you drop the tiny transmitters on your trail — wedging them between cracks in the rock, tossing them onto the floor where mouse droids might pick them up, or dropping them down air shafts.

An hour before dawn, you are heading through an old mine shaft toward Gardulla's pool room when you hear the sound that you've been dreading. In a long tunnel behind you echo the repulsor engines of a seeker droid — a droid shaped like a floating ball, made specifically to hunt down runaway slaves.

Seeker droids have lots of expensive sensors in them — sniffers, DNA sequencers. If this droid has your scent, there's no way that you'll ever escape! It could hunt you all across Tatooine.

Behind the seeker droid, you hear the march of iron feet. Bigger droids are following the seeker, and they'll have ion shielding. There's no way that you can fight battle droids with your Jawa ion blaster.

In desperation, you toss the whole box of transmitters to the ground and run for the pool room. You decide to set the transmitters all off at once, blowing the seeker droid into so many tiny pieces that it can never be repaired.

Your friends run into the pool room. Gardulla is no longer there. You stand for a minute in the doorway, the transmitter in hand, and punch in the command to blow up all of the transmitters at once.

As you do, you see the seeker droid glide around the corner, coming toward you. Its chemo-receptors are extended, and its electronic eye swivels like a searchlight. It lets out a high electronic squeal, telling the backup droids behind that it has spotted you.

Six backup droids rush forward, heavy blaster rifles in hand. They kneel and open fire.

You leap around the doorway. Blaster fire sweeps through the pool room.

Your friends are safely across the room,

climbing up into the air vent. You need to buy some time to escape; you have to time your attack just right. You'd like to destroy the seeker and the backup droids all at once.

You may detonate the transmitter with or without Power.

To destroy the seeker droid and backup droids (without Power): Roll the 20-dice. Your roll# + your skill# + your stealth# is your adventure#.

If your adventure# is equal to or more than 17, add the difference + 35 to your AP total. You timed your attack just right. The seeker droid and the backup droids are destroyed. You may proceed.

If your adventure# is less than 17, but equal to or more than 11, add the difference + 20 to your AP total. You timed your attack a little too late. The backup droids are destroyed, but the seeker droid is still coming. You will have to attack it, either by hand or with the ion blaster (page 59).

If your adventure# is less than 11, subtract the difference from your AP total. You timed your attack early. The seeker droid is destroyed, but the battle droids are still shooting! You run as fast as you can and scurry up into the air vent, where the droids can't reach you. You may proceed.

To destroy the seeker droid and backup droids (using Power)": Choose your Reflex Power. Roll the 20-dice. Your roll# + your skill# + your Power# + your Power's mid-resist# is your adventure#.

If your adventure# is equal to or more than 16, add the difference + 35 to your AP total. You timed your attack just right. The seeker droid and the backup droids behind it are all destroyed. You may proceed.

If your adventure# is less than 16, add the difference + 20 to your AP total. You timed your attack a little too late. The backup droids are destroyed, but the seeker droid is still coming. You will have to attack it, either by hand or with the ion blaster (next page).

To destroy the seeker droid by hand: Roll the 20-dice to pick up a giant scrub brush to use as a club. You chase the seeker droid down and swing at it. Your roll# + your stealth# + your strength# is your adventure#.

If your adventure# is equal to or more than 13, add the difference + 10 to your AP total.

You rush forward with your scrub brush and batter the seeker droid, damaging its repulsor lift. It falls into the pool, where its circuitry explodes. It won't be chasing slaves any more. You may proceed.

If your adventure# is less than 13, subtract the difference from your AP total. The seeker manages to dodge your swings. Choose to either use the ion blaster (below) or go back to "Roll the 20-dice to pick up a giant scrub brush" and repeat until you have defeated the droid.

To destroy the seeker droid with the Jawa ion blaster: Roll the 10-dice to aim. Your roll# + your weapon's long-range# + your weaponry# is your adventure#.

If your adventure# is equal to or more than 6, add the difference + 10 to your AP total. The droid erupts into sparks. It falls into the pool, where its circuitry explodes. It won't be chasing slaves anymore. You may proceed.

If your adventure# is less than 6, subtract the difference from your AP total. You must fire again. Go back to "Roll the 10-dice to aim" and repeat until the droid has been destroyed.

The transmitters that you've been dropping have all exploded. The whole fortress shakes from the fury of it. Smoke fills hallways and corridors, and alarms blare everywhere.

You scurry up into the vent and reach the opening as dawn begins to lighten the skies.

In the distance you see a Jawa sandcrawler rolling over the desert past the fortress, its huge treads creaking. It looks like it is heading toward the rendezvous out by Market Rock. It makes a rumbling noise like distant thunder.

From the upper walls of Gardulla's fortress, a gunner fires a blaster cannon. Perhaps he thinks that the Jawas are coming to attack in full force, given the disturbance that you and your friends have caused.

Blue bolts streak through the night sky and ricochet harmlessly from the heavy armor on the sandcrawler. The sandcrawler lumbers away.

The noise and confusion provide a distraction for you and your friends to make your escape.

You hook yourself to the grappling hook,

and let the fibercord reel out slowly, and then ride to town on your sand skimmers.

You have rescued the Ghostling children and hidden them in Gardulla's pleasure garden. They are safe for the moment, and so are you. Add 300 AP to your AP total.

To read the end of this adventure, please turn to page 114 of your Star Wars Adventures novel, *The Ghostling Children.*